Wish Upon a Friend

It's a wish come true! Read all the books in the Lucky Stars series:

Wish Upon a Friend

by Phoebe Bright
illustrated by Karen Donnelly

SCHOLASTIC INC.

NEW YORK   TORONTO   LONDON   AUCKLAND
SYDNEY   MEXICO CITY   NEW DELHI   HONG KONG

For Elsie Beard, with all my love
Special thanks to Valerie Wilding

ISBN 978-0-545-41998-7

Text copyright © 2012 by Working Partners Limited
Cover art copyright © 2012 by Scholastic Inc.
Interior art copyright © 2012 by Karen Donnelly

12 11 10 9 8 7 6 5 4 3 2 1   12 13 14 15 16 17/0

Printed in China   68
First Scholastic printing, July 2012

Lucky Star that shines so bright,
Who will need your help tonight?
Light up the sky, and thanks to you
Wishes really do come true. . . .

Hello, friend!

I'm Stella Starkeeper, and I want to tell you a secret. Have you ever gazed up at the stars and thought that they could be full of magic? Well, you're right. Stars really are magical!

Their precious starlight allows me to fly down from the sky. I'm always on the lookout for boys and girls who are especially kind and helpful. I train them to become Lucky Stars — people who can make wishes come true!

So next time you're under the twinkling night sky, look out for me. I'll be floating among the stars somewhere.

Give me a wave!

Love,

Stella Starkeeper

"Whee!" cried Cassie.

"Whoa!" shouted her mom.

The spinning teacup ride whirled so fast, the blue of the sea and sky blurred into the bright fairground colors.

When the ride stopped, Mom took a deep, shaky breath.

Cassie giggled. "We'll try something slower next," she said. She felt a little bit dizzy, too!

Mom tottered out of the teacup. "It's your birthday," she said. "You can choose whatever ride you want."

Cassie couldn't help thinking about how lucky she was to live in Astral-on-Sea. Her home, Starwatcher Towers, was on top of a cliff that overlooked the whole town and the beach, too. Even though she had no brothers or sisters to play with, there was always so much to do — exploring rock pools, collecting pretty shells, building sandcastles . . . and now the Fun Fair had arrived in town! Cassie thought the rides were even more fun than the birthday party she'd had yesterday.

"What should we try next?" asked Mom. "The scrambler? Or the bumper cars?"

Cassie couldn't decide. Then she spotted a small tent, glistening silver in the sunshine. A sequined curtain covered the entrance, with a sign above it that read:

Lucky Dip!

"What's a lucky dip?" asked Cassie.

"It's a box of surprises," explained her mom with a smile. "You close your eyes, put your hand inside, and pull out a gift."

"I like the sound of that!" said Cassie.

As they reached the tent, she noticed a small bell next to the entrance with a rope of silvery stars dangling from it. She peered around the curtain. Inside, a woman in a long cloak was sitting next to a wooden box.

Cassie had the strangest feeling that she needed to enter the silver tent. She turned to her mom. "Can I go in, please?"

Mom took a coin from her purse and nodded. "Give this to the lady. I'll wait here."

Cassie slipped the coin into her pocket. Gently, she pulled the rope of stars outside the tent and jangled the bell.

* ✳ ★ ✳

"Come in," called the woman in a warm, clear voice.

Cassie's stomach fluttered as she pushed the sequined curtain aside. The tent was lit by clusters of glass ornaments that dangled on sparkling threads. She could see her blonde hair and brown eyes dancing on the shiny surfaces.

"They're so pretty!" Cassie breathed. "My bedroom has a glass ceiling, and your ornaments remind me of the stars I see at night. I live in an observatory, since my dad studies the night sky," she continued. "I'm even named after the stars."

The woman smiled. "Cassiopeia is my favorite constellation," she said.

Cassie blinked. "That's my name!" she

said. Her parents had named her after the group of stars known as Cassiopeia. "How did you know?"

"A lucky guess," replied the woman.

Her cloak was the color of the moonlit sky, and a matching scarf was draped over her head and face. A lock of silver-blonde hair rippled across her shoulder. Cassie sat in the chair across from her, where she could see her eyes. They were a deep, velvety blue and sparkled like stars.

"Happy birthday," the woman said in her soft voice. "Seven is a very special age, you know."

Cassie's mouth fell open in surprise. "How do you know it's my birthday? And how do you know I'm seven?" she asked. "You must be very good at guessing."

"Perhaps," the woman said. Her eyes twinkled. "Look."

She lifted the lid of the wooden box. It was full of tiny silver stars, shining like Christmas lights.

Cassie gasped. They looked magical!

"Many things are hidden among these stars," the woman said. "One of them is yours. Can you find it?"

Cassie dipped her hand into the box. The stars rustled as she searched among them. Her fingers closed over something solid, and she felt a shiver run up her arm. *This must be it*, she thought, pulling out a delicate silver chain.

"Wonderful! I knew you'd find your bracelet," said the woman.

"*My* bracelet? What do you mean?" Cassie asked. "I've never seen it before."

The woman fastened the bracelet onto Cassie's wrist and winked. "You'll find out before your birthday is over," she said. "And now you must go."

Cassie admired the delicate silver bracelet. "I love it," she said. "Thank you so much. Good-bye!"

"Good-bye," said the woman, "for now . . ."

Outside in the sunshine, Cassie couldn't wait to show her mom the bracelet.

"That's awfully nice," Mom said, studying it. "Are you sure she meant for you to keep it, though?"

"Yes," answered Cassie. "She said it was mine."

Suddenly, there was a squeal from the beach. A donkey was nibbling at a woman's beach chair! The woman was flapping her towel at the donkey, trying to shoo it away.

"Look!" Cassie cried. "Bert needs help."

Bert worked on the boardwalk, and Cassie loved to visit him. He had a cotton candy stall, plus six donkeys that kids could ride on the beach. But now one of the donkeys, Coco, had wandered away!

Cassie ran across the sand and gave Coco a hug. He was new and a little nervous, but he was getting braver every day.

"You'll be best friends with the other

donkeys soon, Coco," Cassie whispered as she led him back to the others.

Bert's wrinkled brown face broke into a grin. "Thanks, Cassie," he said, looking relieved. "And happy birthday!"

"Thank you!" Cassie waved good-bye and ran back to where her mom was waiting.

"Nice job, birthday girl! It's time for some cake now." Mom grinned. "Then I need to get the B&B ready for our new guests."

Part of Starwatcher Towers was Mom's bed-and-breakfast. Visitors to Astral-on-Sea came to stay in the guest rooms, and Cassie's mom made a big breakfast for them every morning. Dad worked in the other part—the observatory. His job was to study

the stars and planets. Today, though, he was in the kitchen, frosting Cassie's birthday cake. Every year he decorated it differently.

Cassie started to skip home, thinking about biting into a delicious piece of birthday cake, but something fell from her pocket and plopped onto the sand. It was the coin Mom had given her for the woman in the silver tent. "Oh, no! I forgot to pay!" Cassie looked anxiously at her mom.

"Don't worry. We'll take it to her on our way home," Mom said.

But no matter how hard they looked, they couldn't find the little silver tent anywhere. *It's completely vanished*, thought Cassie. *Like magic.*

★ ★ ★

★ ✳ ★ ✳

That night before bed, Cassie had one last
sliver of cake. This year, Dad had iced it with
a shower of shooting stars in all different
colors.

"It's not what stars really look like," he'd
said, "but it's pretty."

"It's beautiful!" Cassie and Mom had both
said together.

At bedtime, Cassie took her presents
upstairs. Her old cat, Twinkle, was already
snoozing on the pillow.

Cassie loved her room. Since it was in one of the towers, it was almost completely round. On clear nights, she would lie in bed and gaze up through the glass ceiling at the stars. With her moon-shaped lamp casting a soft glow on her starry wallpaper, and the real stars overhead, Cassie liked to imagine she was drifting through the sky. (And when it rained, it was like being under a waterfall without getting wet!)

Cassie changed into her purple star pajamas and started to take her bracelet off. *No*, she decided. *I'll keep it on. It will remind me of my wonderful day!*

Cassie jumped into bed, then leaned over and thumped twice on the floor. That was her special signal to let Mom and Dad know that she was ready to go to sleep. When they came in, Mom told her that the new guests at the B&B had a son her age. "You'll see him tomorrow," she promised.

Cassie kissed Dad good night. "Thank you for a great birthday—and the yummy cake."

Just as Mom leaned down to kiss Cassie good night, Dad gave a yell, making them all jump.

"Look!" he cried, pointing up through the glass ceiling. "A meteor shower! I wasn't expecting this!"

Cassie scrambled to sit up. "Wow!" she said. The sky was filled with streaks of light. She knew they were really meteors—glowing trails left by bits of space dust or rocks—but

she preferred to call them shooting stars. After all, that's what they looked like! As she watched them flash against the dark sky, she felt a tingle of excitement.

"How strange," said Mom. "There was a meteor shower just like this the night you were born, Cassie."

Dad rubbed his hands together. "Forget about bed! Let's go to the observatory and watch the meteor shower through my telescopes," he said.

Cassie usually jumped at the chance to look at the sky through Dad's telescopes, but tonight, for some reason, she wanted to watch the shooting stars by herself. "I think Twinkle and I will watch from here," she said. "Dad, can you open one of the panels, please?"

He turned a lever and a section of the glass ceiling swung open, letting in the cool night air. Then he gave Cassie a kiss and hurried to the observatory with Mom.

Cassie snuggled under the blankets and glanced down at her bracelet. What she saw made her gasp. It was fizzing with tiny silver sparkles!

"Wow! Why's it doing that, Twinkle?" she asked her cuddly old cat.

But Twinkle was staring up at the sky. His fur stood on end and his tail flicked. Suddenly, he yowled, leaped onto the floor, and dived under the bed.

Cassie looked up to see what had scared him. One shooting star, bigger than the rest, was swirling downward. It came closer and closer.

And it seemed to be heading right for Cassie!

2

Stella Starkeeper

With a *whizz* and a *fizz* and a *zip-zip-zip*, the star shot through the open glass panel, showering the room with silver sparkles.

Cassie was so astonished that she couldn't even move. What was happening?

The star slowed and hovered just above the rug. Cassie stared as it grew into a column of dazzling light, which slowly changed into a pretty, young woman. She was dressed all in silver and wore a shiny cropped jacket with star-shaped buttons on the cuffs. Her short dress rippled over glittery leggings and shiny boots. In her hand was a wand, tipped with a twinkling star. The woman's crown was woven from delicate strands of silver, and her blonde hair shone in the starlight. As she smiled, her velvety blue eyes sparkled.

Cassie had seen those eyes before. "You gave me the bracelet!" she cried.

"I did," said the woman in her soft voice. "My name is Stella Starkeeper. And who's this?"

Twinkle had creeped out from under the bed. As Stella tickled his chin, Cassie noticed that Stella wore a bracelet just like hers, but with charms hanging from it.

The old cat purred and tapped the wand

with his paw. A shower of silver glitter floated
down to the rug.

"Does all this have something to do with
my bracelet?" Cassie asked. "Is it magical?"

Stella took her hand. "It is," she said,

smiling. "Now, would you like to see some more magic?"

Cassie nodded and, with a *whoosh*, found herself flying up through the open window with Stella. "Oh!" she cried, clutching Stella's hand. She felt as light as a balloon as they circled the treetops, floating high in the night sky.

Up and up they soared. Cassie looked down and saw a light in Dad's observatory. Could he see her through his telescope? What would he think? The thought made laughter bubble up inside of her.

They left the lights of Astral-on-Sea far below as Stella took Cassie higher and higher. Soon, they were flying among the stars.

"They're all different colors," said Cassie, looking around in awe. "Violet and gold, orange and scarlet. And they're playing together!"

The stars danced and bobbed all around them. Cassie watched a tiny pink star chase a little blue one in circles. They reminded her of kittens scampering around a tree! Suddenly, the pink star skidded and tumbled toward her.

"The poor thing can't stop," Cassie cried. She reached out and gently patted the pink star back toward its little blue friend. As it bobbed around happily again, Stella waved her wand.

Cassie felt her wrist tingle. She looked down to see a tiny bird charm dangling from her bracelet.

Sparkles swirled all around her, and she realized that something amazing had happened. Stella wasn't holding her hand anymore.

"I'm flying!" she gasped. "All by myself!"

For a moment Cassie was afraid, but when Stella smiled, she smiled back. With a shiver of excitement, Cassie tumbled through the air in a forward somersault, feeling as free as a bird.

"Am I like you, Stella?" she wondered out loud. "I can fly now, and I have a bracelet like yours."

Stella flew alongside Cassie as they moved between the bright, bobbing stars. "Would you like that?" she asked. "Would you like to become a *real* Lucky Star?"

"Oh, yes!" said Cassie. Then she paused to think. "But what does that mean?"

"Lucky Stars use their magic to make other people's wishes come true," Stella explained, her blonde hair swirling behind her.

Cassie grinned. "Then I *definitely* want to become a Lucky Star! But how?"

"Just by being yourself," said Stella. "I chose you because you can't resist helping people—just like you helped that tiny pink star." She touched Cassie's bracelet. "This bird charm is the first step in your Lucky Star training. It gives you the power to fly."

They swooped away as a bunch of lime green stars danced around their heads. Then Cassie turned back to Stella, listening carefully. She couldn't believe her ears!

"To become a Lucky Star, you must always watch and listen for someone to make a wish—someone who really deserves your help," Stella continued. "If you make their wish come true, you'll get another charm, which will give you a new magical power. Once you've collected seven charms, you'll be a Lucky Star." She smiled at Cassie. "And Lucky Stars don't have to wait for somebody

★　　✳　　★　　✳

to make a wish. They can grant wishes whenever they like!"

That sounded amazing—no, magical!—to Cassie.

As Stella slowly floated downward, Cassie followed. She looked out at the sea, sparkling in the moonlight. "Almost home," she said. Stella waved her wand, and Cassie suddenly felt sleepy. Her eyes closed for a moment. "Almost . . . home . . ."

When Cassie opened her eyes again, she was back in her bed. Stella was gone. She snuggled under her quilt, and Twinkle settled down next to her.

"I'll be a Lucky Star one day, Twinkle," she whispered. "I'm going to do my best to make wishes come true."

The old cat purred, and Cassie closed her eyes.

"I wonder who I'll be helping first," she murmured. "I can't wait until tomorrow!"

★ 3 ★
Alex and Comet

Sizzle, hiss, sizzle!

"Mmm," Cassie murmured. She stretched and sniffed. Bacon! Mom was cooking breakfast.

Cassie quickly brushed her teeth and got dressed, wondering what the new guests were like. She hoped their son was nice!

As she went downstairs, her bracelet jangled against the banister. She peered at the bird charm and suddenly remembered her adventure the night before. "I flew!" she said out loud. "Or was that just a dream?"

No one was around, so Cassie decided to do a test.

She stood on the bottom step, squeezed her eyes shut, and thought about her bird charm. Instantly, she felt herself floating upward. As she opened her eyes, she saw that she was

drifting gently down the hallway toward the kitchen. Sparkles shimmered around her bracelet.

"It was real!" she cried, floating back down onto the carpet.

Mom popped her head out of the kitchen. "What was real?"

Cassie hesitated. She didn't think Mom would believe her if she explained about Stella or her new bird charm. She could hardly believe it herself!

"Nothing," Cassie said at last. She pointed to her old cat, who was settling on his cushion next to the hall radiator. "I was talking to Twinkle."

"Well, head into the dining room and talk to the guests," said Mom. "I'm just about to bring breakfast out."

A man, a woman, and a boy with curly brown hair were sitting at the long wooden table in the dining room.

"Hi," said Cassie.

The woman smiled. "You must be Cassie. This is our son, Alex," she said. "And that's Comet, under the table."

Under the table? Cassie bent down and saw a small, fluffy white puppy chewing a blue rubber bone. He wagged his tail.

Twinkle won't like Comet staying here! she thought. But she had to admit that Comet was awfully cute.

Alex seemed to be concentrating on a box in his lap. Cassie glanced at it and saw test tubes inside. "What's that?" she asked.

Alex fidgeted. "Well, er . . . actually, it's top secret," he said.

"Show Cassie," said his dad. "I'm sure she won't tell anyone."

"Of course not," said Cassie.

"It's my experiment," Alex told her. "I'm going to be a scientist when I grow up."

"Are you really?" Cassie was interested. "What's the experiment for?"

Alex tapped a notebook that lay beside his cereal bowl. "It's all in here," he said, "but it's easier to show you." He held a test tube over the bowl. "The white powder in here is baking soda, and I'm going to add some of this green food coloring. Could you get me some vinegar, please?"

Cassie headed to the kitchen, grabbed the bottle from one of the cabinets, and brought it back to Alex.

"Watch," said Alex as he poured some into the test tube.

The mixture fizzed and bubbled into a green froth that erupted into the bowl.

"Wow!" said Cassie. "That's like magic!"

"It's not magic," said Alex, shrugging his shoulders. "It's science." He jotted down some notes. "These are my observations."

"You'd get along well with my dad," said Cassie. "He's an astronomer."

Alex's father grinned. "We're on vacation here for two weeks, so I'm sure Alex would love to see your dad's observatory."

Cassie gave Alex a smile, but he just kept writing in his notebook. Cassie's mom hurried in with enormous plates of bacon, eggs, sausage, fruit, and toast, but Cassie decided just to have a piece of toast and leave. Alex didn't seem all that friendly, and besides, she wanted to see if what Stella had said about becoming a Lucky Star was true. It sounded so exciting!

I wonder who has a special wish, she thought, as she took a bite of her toast. *And how can I make it come true?*

4
Helping Bert

"Excuse me," Cassie said to Alex's family. "I'm going out now." She reached down to pet the cute little puppy. "Bye, Comet."

As she stood up, she accidentally bumped the edge of the table, making the cups and plates rattle. "Oops!" she said. Two apples toppled from the fruit bowl.

Cassie caught one, and just before the other rolled off the table, Alex grabbed it.

He passed it to her. "Here you go."

"You moved fast!" said Cassie. "Thanks."

He smiled, then quickly looked down.

Oh! He's not unfriendly, thought Cassie suddenly. *He's shy!*

"Would you like to come to the beach?" she asked him.

Alex's face lit up. "Really?" he said. He carefully put his experiment off to one side of the dining room. Then he grinned, as if he couldn't wait to get going. "Can we take Comet?" he asked.

"Yes," said his dad, "but don't let him run off."

"We won't, I promise," said Cassie.

Alex clipped a leash to Comet's collar, and they stepped out into the morning sunshine. Cassie noticed Twinkle lounging in the garden, enjoying the sun. But when he spotted the puppy, he scuttled under the hedge.

"Ruff! Ruff!" Comet barked. He pulled on his leash, trying to reach the cat.

"He just wants to play," said Alex.

"But he's scaring Twinkle," said Cassie. "Don't worry," she told her cat. "Comet's just visiting for a while."

As they walked down the hill toward the beach, Comet ran ahead. His body moved too quickly for his legs, and he kept tumbling over.

"He's so cute," said Cassie. "And fast! Comets are actually just frozen dust and gas, but they travel around the sun at thousands of miles an hour. So Comet's a good name for him!"

"That's interesting," said Alex. "You know lots about stars and planets, don't you?"

Cassie nodded. "My dad tells me all about them." She suddenly realized that now she knew things about stars her dad didn't even know—how they liked to play, for instance. She'd even touched one!

When they reached the part of the beach where dogs were allowed, Cassie and Alex jumped off the low wall onto the warm sand. Comet sniffed the salty sea air and barked with excitement.

As they wandered along, Cassie looked around, trying to find someone who needed her help. But everybody seemed perfectly happy! Couples snoozed in beach chairs. Kids dug in the sand or splashed in the rippling waves. A toddler was crying in the ice cream line on the boardwalk, but his dad was about to place his order. He didn't need her help!

Up ahead, a woman struggled to push her stroller across the sand. As it bumped along, a small blue teddy bear fell out. Cassie ran to pick up the bear and give it back to the baby, who giggled and clapped his hands.

Immediately, Cassie checked her bracelet. The bird charm dangled there, all by itself. *I guess the baby wasn't really wishing for my help,* thought Cassie. *But I'm glad I made him happy.*

"*Ruff! Ruff!*" Comet peered at Bert's line of donkeys and riders, way down near the water's edge.

"Stay!" said Alex. But it was clear that Comet wanted to meet the donkeys. He yelped and pulled and suddenly he was gone, his leash trailing behind him!

"Quick, after him!" shouted Cassie. "If he frightens the donkeys, they'll bolt and the kids could fall off."

The soft sand made it difficult to run.

"We won't catch him in time," Cassie panted. "Poor Coco the donkey will be so scared!" Her bracelet jingled as she ran, and she remembered her bird charm. *Oh*, she thought, *I wonder . . .*

Instantly, she tingled all over. Tiny silver

sparkles danced around her bracelet. Then Cassie felt herself rise a little, so her feet were just above the sand! She floated past Alex and caught up with Comet in no time, grabbing his leash.

"Got him!" she called.

She saw Alex giving her a strange look. *Flying's my special secret*, Cassie thought. *I'm not ready to tell anyone about it yet.*

Quickly, she curled into a forward somersault on the sand, hoping Alex would think she'd just done a spectacular acrobatic move.

Alex picked up Comet and turned to Bert. "Sorry——" he began, but Bert was looking back at his cotton candy stall on the boardwalk. He frowned.

"What's wrong?" Cassie asked.

"My son should be selling cotton candy today," said Bert, "but he's at home with a cold. I'm tired of going from the donkeys to the cotton candy and back again. It's hard to keep an eye on everything." He sighed.

Cassie's heart leaped. It sounded like Bert was wishing for help! "I'll do it!" she said. "I'll make the cotton candy for you."

Bert's eyes lit up, but then he said, "A little thing like you, making cotton candy?"

"Why not?" said Cassie. She saw Alex fidget, hopping from foot to foot, almost as if he wanted to be noticed. Of course! "I won't be on my own," she told Bert. "You'll help too, won't you, Alex?"

A grin spread across Alex's face.

"All right, then," said Bert, "but come and get me if you have any problems."

Cassie grabbed Alex's hand and they raced to the cotton candy stall. Alex walked Comet over to the shade and looped his leash over a post. He filled a metal bowl with fresh water from the tap and put it next to his puppy.

Behind the counter, Cassie studied the whirring cotton candy machine and the heap of sugar glistening like starlight. She looked out at the growing line of kids. Then she looked back at the cotton candy machine.

"Alex," she said, "I promised Bert I'd help, but—I don't know how!"

5

Going Up!

"What should we do?" Cassie asked, worried.

"Let's see." Alex peered at the machine. "The heater warms the sugar . . . turns it into liquid . . . spins the liquid . . ."

"Excuse me!" called a girl's voice.

Cassie had to stretch to see over the high counter. A pretty girl with wavy hair and sky blue eyes was second in the line, and she tapped her foot impatiently. Cassie ducked down.

* ✳ ★ ✳

"It's Donna Fox," she whispered to Alex, wrinkling her nose. "Her parents own the Flashley Manor Hotel. She's spoiled rotten."

"*Excuse* me!" the voice said again.

Cassie stood on her tiptoes. "Hi, Donna," she said, doing her best to smile.

"The cotton candy will be ready soon."

"I certainly hope so!" said Donna. Her eyes narrowed. "Are you sure you know what you're doing?"

"I have an expert here," said Cassie,

bending down again. "That's you, Alex. Hurry up!"

"I won't wait forever," Donna called. "I could always just buy my cotton candy somewhere else."

I wish you would, Cassie thought, almost missing what Alex was saying.

". . . out come thousands of threads, and you twirl them on a stick," he finished "Easy!"

Cassie poured sugar into the container in the middle of the machine, then Alex added pink food coloring. The container rattled and whirled, and out flew pale pink threads of spun sugar.

"Alex, I need a stick!" cried Cassie

Alex swiftly handed her one. Cassie twirled it around and around inside the bowl, and watched a pink cloud begin to form. When it was as big as her head, she stretched over the counter to pass it to the boy at the front of the line.

But Donna Fox reached across and snatched it right out of Cassie's hand! She flung her money on the counter and stalked away.

"Hey!" the boy shouted. "That's mine."

"Don't worry," said Cassie, scooping up

Donna's coins. "I'll make an extra-big one for you."

Alex was busy taking money and refilling the machine, so Cassie kept twirling spun sugar onto the sticks. But it was hard to reach the smaller kids over the high counter! She glanced down. Her feet were hidden by sugar bags, so she thought about her bird charm. Silver sparkles danced around her bracelet, and her feet left the ground! Cassie rose just high enough to reach the machine and the kids easily.

Alex opened a fresh bag of sugar and poured it into the machine. He looked up at Cassie. "You seem taller."

"I'm on my tiptoes," said Cassie.

Outside the booth, one little girl stood back

from the others. Cassie thought she looked
scared.

"Your turn, Rosie," a tall
girl said to her. "Come on.
The puppy won't hurt you."

Alex called across the
counter. "Comet's very
friendly."

Rosie shook her head
and stayed still.

"I know!" said Cassie.
"Let's make Rosie a special
batch of cotton candy.
She'll have to be brave and go past Comet if
she wants it. Put extra coloring in, Alex."

He poured in double the usual amount.
Soon, Cassie was twirling a deep pink cloud

of cotton candy. She held it out. "Here, Rosie. It's rose colored to match your name!"

Was it her imagination, or did the cotton candy stick tug at her fingers—like it was trying to break free?

Rosie's eyes widened. She took a deep breath, then edged past Comet to take the treat from Cassie. "Thanks!"

Cassie smiled as she twirled another stick. Her plan had worked! But then she heard Rosie give a startled cry.

She looked up to see Rosie's cotton candy starting to rise into the air. Up it went, taking the little girl with it!

"What's happening?" Rosie squealed.

"Alex, quick!" cried Cassie. They ran around to where Rosie bobbed beneath her pink cotton-candy cloud. Luckily, no one else seemed to have noticed Rosie yet! Alex and Cassie each grabbed one of her dangling legs.

"There must be a scientific reason for this," Alex yelled, "if I can just figure it out."

Cassie knew the reason. Tiny silver sparkles danced all around the cotton candy. They swirled down the stick and around Rosie, then over Alex and Cassie, too. Somehow the charm's magic had spread!

Oh, no! thought Cassie. *I'll have to be much more careful with my magic from now on.*

Cassie cried, "Pull Rosie down!"

But they couldn't. Instead, she and Alex began to rise, too. As they floated past Comet, the puppy jumped up and caught the leg of Alex's jeans between his teeth. Up they floated, bobbing gently in the breeze. Cassie looked down to see the puppy's leash slide off the top of the post.

"Comet's coming with us," she called to Alex as silver sparkles swirled toward the small white puppy. She looked up, hoping Rosie wasn't too frightened, but the little girl was busy trying to catch sparkles with her free hand.

They flew higher and higher, the cotton candy at the top, then Rosie, then Cassie and Alex hanging on to her legs. Comet was last, holding Alex's jeans in his mouth. And they

were *all* surrounded by sparkly magic!

Cassie tried not to look down as they drifted higher in the sky. She squeezed her eyes shut and gulped. *How in the world am I going to fix this?* Cassie wondered in dismay.

6

Cotton Candy and Clouds

They soared even higher, until Astral-on-Sea looked like a tiny toy town below them. Even though it was daytime, Cassie could see the faint glimmer of stars and the pale shimmer of the crescent moon.

She felt something brush past her hair—a fluffy blob of cotton candy had come loose!

Alex saw it, too. First his eyes opened wide in surprise . . . and then his mouth opened! He leaned forward and took a bite. "Mmmm," he said with a grin.

Cassie was too worried to smile back. She looked up. "Are you okay, Rosie?" But the face that looked down was smiling. "This is fun!" squealed Rosie with delight. "Look!" Alex pointed to a puffy white cloud moving past. "It has a flat bottom and bumpy top, like cauliflower—it's a cumulus cloud."

Cassie sighed. Of course Alex was studying the clouds when they should be trying to get back down to the beach!

Something white and fluffy drifted past her nose. At first she thought it was a little cloud, but then she saw the wagging tail. "Comet!" she cried.

The puppy had let go of Alex's jeans and now bobbed around Rosie. The little girl giggled, then reached out and hugged him close. "We're flying together," Cassie heard her tell Comet.

Hooray! thought Cassie. *At least Rosie isn't scared of dogs anymore!*

Alex was still busy cloud-spotting. "That cumulus is evaporating," he said. "See? It's getting wispy and disappearing."

"The cotton candy is getting wispy, too," said Cassie, as they all took a dip downward. Suddenly, she had an idea. "Rosie—let's find out what your cotton candy tastes like!"

Rosie reached up and pulled away a handful of spun sugar. She popped it into her mouth. "It tastes . . . magical!" she said. She tore off two more pieces and passed them down. Cassie took a bite. The cotton candy melted on her tongue like sugary snowflakes. Rosie pulled off more pieces for all of them. As the stick of cotton candy became smaller, the silver sparkles began to fade. They drifted down.

My plan worked, thought Cassie happily.

Astral-on-Sea grew larger again, and soon they had all landed safely back on the sand.

Rosie hugged Cassie. "Thanks!" she said. "That was a fantastic adventure." She patted Comet. "And thank you, Comet! I won't be scared of dogs anymore if they're all as nice as you!"

A group of children gathered around, chatting and grinning excitedly.

"Rosie, you flew!" said a boy.

Before Rosie could speak, Alex said, "It wasn't exactly flying, you know."

"It sure looked like it," said the tall girl.

"No, it has to do with changes in air pressure," said Alex. "Have you heard of thermal columns? Warm air expands, you see, and it rises. . . ."

Cassie smiled. Thank goodness for Alex's scientific mind. He hadn't guessed there was magic in the air at all. The bracelet's secret was safe!

"I'd better get back to my mom now," said Rosie. "Bye!" She'd only taken two steps when she bent to pick something up. It was a piece of hard, shiny driftwood, almost as round as a ball. "This is for Comet to play with," she said.

The puppy wagged his tail, and tried to take the ball in his mouth. It was too big, so he pushed it with his nose. The kids all laughed and headed off in different directions.

Just then, Bert walked up to the cotton candy stall, leading Coco the donkey. "Thank you for helping me today, Cassie," he said. "Did you have fun?"

"Oh, yes!" cried Cassie. She was relieved that Bert hadn't spotted them flying through the air! "We had a great afternoon. Now it's time for us to go home."

Alex carried Comet's present, and the three of them headed up the hill toward Starwatcher Towers. Cassie couldn't stop smiling. She'd helped Bert with the cotton candy, *and* she'd helped Rosie get over her fear of dogs.

Her heart skipped a beat. She'd helped two people, hadn't she? Then maybe . . . ? She spun her bracelet around on her wrist.

But there was no new charm.

7

All Together

"What's so interesting about that bracelet?" Alex asked. "You keep looking at it."

"It's hard to explain," Cassie said. "All I can say is that it's important for me to help people—like I helped Rosie not be afraid of dogs."

Alex frowned. "What does the bracelet have to do with that?" he asked.

Cassie changed the subject. "Look, we're

home." She opened the gate. "Let's see if Mom's been baking."

Alex unclipped the puppy's leash and dropped his driftwood ball. Comet's tail wagged madly. *"Ruff! Ruff!"*

"He's scaring Twinkle!" said Cassie.

In the nearby garden, the cat arched his back. His fur stood up like brush bristles.

Comet wasn't afraid of him. He nudged the driftwood ball with his nose. It rolled toward Twinkle. When it stopped, the cat reached out a paw to pat it.

"He likes it," whispered Cassie.

Comet dashed forward and pushed the ball again. This time, Twinkle chased it and batted it with his paw.

"They're playing," said Cassie. "I can't believe it! Twinkle doesn't usually like strangers."

Alex watched the puppy and the cat chase the ball around the garden. "They're not strangers anymore — they're friends." He looked down, scuffing the grass with his shoe. "I wish I had a new friend, too."

Cassie remembered how she'd thought Alex was unfriendly at first, but now she knew he was just shy. She was about to say something when it dawned on her—Alex had made a wish. And she was making it come true!

She grinned. "You *do* have a new friend," she said. "Me!"

Alex looked up and gave Cassie an enormous smile.

"Wait here," said Cassie. She ran into the kitchen, where she found trays of freshly baked cookies. Cassie took two cookies out to the garden. "One for me, and the biggest one for you," she said to Alex, "to celebrate our friendship."

A tingle ran up her arm.

"Huh?" Alex pointed to her wrist.

Her bracelet was glowing!

"Wow!" Cassie was so excited to see a new charm appear there—a crescent moon! Its beautiful shimmer reminded her of the real moon she'd seen as they flew among the clouds.

Alex's eyes widened. "What's happening?" He looked at the bracelet, then at Cassie.

She decided to let Alex in on her secret.

He was her friend, after all. "Sit down, and I'll tell you all about it. It's not science — it's magic!"

She explained about Stella Starkeeper, and how the charms were part of becoming a Lucky Star.

"They help me make wishes come true." Cassie looked at her new charm. "The bird charm gave me the power to fly, and we had such a good time up in the clouds that now we're friends — and your wish came true!"

They nibbled their cookies quietly for a moment, watching Comet and Twinkle play with the driftwood ball.

"So we really *were* flying?" said Alex.

"Yes, really." Cassie smiled. "It must be hard for you to believe in magic."

He nodded, looking thoughtful. "I'm used to finding logical explanations," he said. Cassie nudged him. "Well, you can use your super-scientific brain to help me make the next person's wish come true."

Twinkle was carefully licking Comet's floppy ears clean.

"I'm really glad you and Comet are staying at Starwatcher Towers," said Cassie.

Alex grinned. "Me, too!"

★ ★ ★

Later, when Mom and Dad had kissed Cassie good night, she slipped out of bed and

picked up Twinkle.
She rose with him
toward her glass
ceiling and floated
there, gazing at
the stars.

"Who will make a
wish next, Twinkle?"
she wondered. "And what
power does my new moon charm have?"

As she drifted down to bed, the soft, clear
voice of Stella Starkeeper floated across the
twinkling sky. "Good night, Lucky Star!"

Make Your Own!

You can make your own sparkly star wand, just like Stella Starkeeper's! Here's how:

You Need:
- A pencil
- Scissors
- A piece of sturdy cardboard
- Glue
- One wooden dowel rod, about 12 inches long
- Silver aluminum foil
- Ribbon in your favorite color

★ ✳ ★ ✳

1. Draw a star on the cardboard and cut it out. Using that star as a stencil, trace it on the remaining cardboard and cut it out, so you have two identical cardboard stars.

2. Lay one star facedown and spread glue on the side that's facing you. Place your wooden dowel flat in the center of the star, with 10 inches of the dowel sticking out the bottom. Place your other star on top and push, so it sticks to the glue on the bottom star.

3. Take a sheet of silver aluminum foil and wrap it around the star, molding it to fit.

4. Finish your wand by tying a ribbon below the star, or wrapping it around the dowel. Now you're a Lucky Star!

Cassie's magical adventures are just
beginning! Can she make another wish
come true? Take a sneak peek at

#2: Wish Upon a Pet!

1

Stella Starkeeper

"Wow! That wind is strong!" Cassie said. She laughed as a star-patterned pillowcase blew off the clothesline and into her face.

The two charms on Cassie's silver bracelet jangled as she hung the pillowcase back on the line. She glanced at the charms—a tiny bird and a crescent moon—and smiled. Their magic helped her make special wishes come true! *I hope I meet someone with a wish today,* she thought.

"When we offered to help your mom hang up the laundry, I didn't expect to have to chase it around the yard!" called her friend Alex.

Cassie looked up to see him collecting three socks that had blown into an apple tree. She laughed.

The catflap in the back door clattered. Out ran Alex's fluffy white puppy, Comet, followed by Cassie's cat, Twinkle. The pets had become friends, too—just like Cassie and Alex!

Cassie stroked Twinkle's black fur.

"Meowwww," he yowled.

"Ruff!" barked Comet.

Cassie brushed her long hair out of her eyes. "You two should stay inside," she told the animals. "You might blow away!"

"Only if the wind's strong enough," said Alex, stroking his chin. "I'll get my anemometer, so I can measure the wind speed." He ran inside. The wind banged the door shut behind him.

Cassie threw another towel over the line. As she held it down with a clothespin, she noticed a bright light shining through the clouds overhead. *Is that a star?* Cassie wondered. *In the morning?*

Cassie's dad had taught her a lot about the stars. She knew that you couldn't usually see them in daytime, because the sun was too bright. But as she watched, this star seemed to be whirling down toward her!

Cassie remembered the last time she saw a star doing something like that. Could it be . . . ?

With a *whoosh* and a *whiz* and a *fizz-fizz-fizz*, the star was suddenly next to her in a flurry of silver sparkles. It grew into a column of dazzling light and then changed into —

"Stella Starkeeper!" cried Cassie. "You're back!"